Afrotina and the Three Bears

TO SOW THE FALLOW SOIL

Winston-Derek Publishers, Inc.
Pennywell Drive—P.O. Box 90883
Nashville, TN 37209

Copyright 1991 by Winston-Derek Publishers, Inc.

All rights reserved. No part of this book may be reproduced in any form without written permission from the publishers, except by a reviewer who may quote brief passages in a review to be printed in a newspaper or magazine.

First printing

PUBLISHED BY WINSTON-DEREK PUBLISHERS, INC.
Nashville, Tennessee 37205

Library of Congress Catalog Card No: 88-51222
ISBN: 1-55523-195-0

Printed in the United States of America

For
Amber and Kristen
or
Kristen and Amber

Afrotina and the Three Bears

Retold and Illustrated by
Fred Crump, Jr.

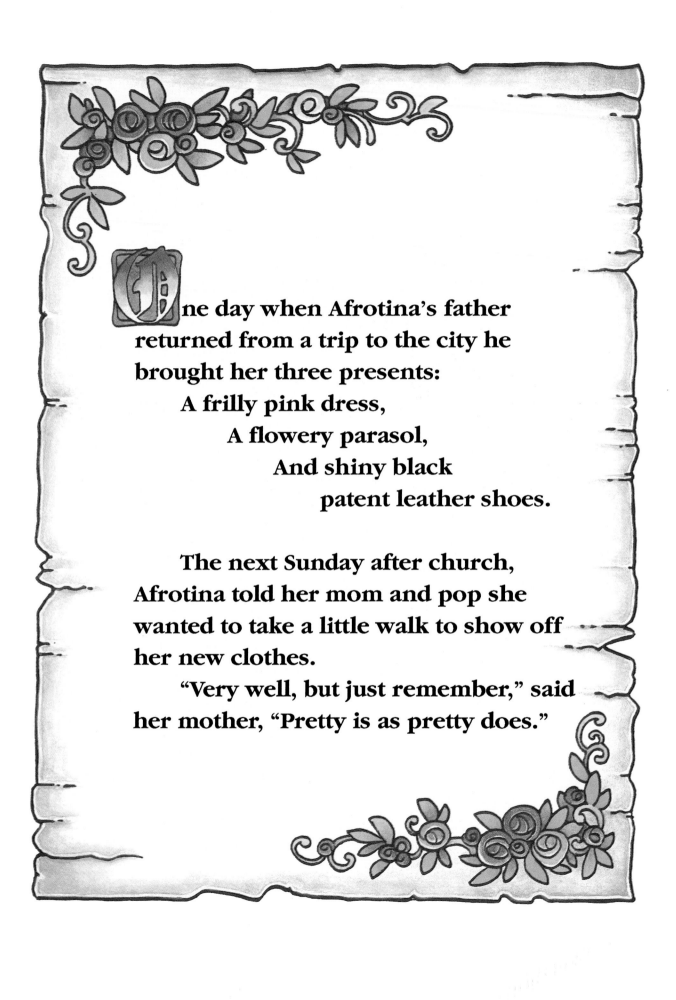

One day when Afrotina's father returned from a trip to the city he brought her three presents:
A frilly pink dress,
A flowery parasol,
And shiny black
patent leather shoes.

The next Sunday after church, Afrotina told her mom and pop she wanted to take a little walk to show off her new clothes.

"Very well, but just remember," said her mother, "Pretty is as pretty does."

AFROTINA HAS A NEW DRESS

And Afrotina skipped off, twirling her flowery parasol.

AFROTINA SKIPPED ON THE PATH

efore long she came to a cave in the woods. It was the home of the three bears who were out for a walk while their soup cooled.

"Yum! Something in there smells good," said Afrotina. Then, without a knock or "Hello" she went into the cave.

SHE DIDN'T KNOCK AT THE DOOR

The table was set with three bowls of soup. Afrotina sat on Papa Bear's chair. It was too high. Then she sat on Mama Bear's chair. It was too low. Then she sat on Baby Bear's chair . . .

. . . and it broke all to pieces.

WHOOPS! THE CHAIR BROKE!

So she stood up at the table and tasted Papa Bear's soup. "Whooee!" It was too hot.

Then she tried Mama Bear's soup. "Yuck!" It was too salty.

Then she tasted Baby Bear's soup. "Yummy!" It was just right. And she ate it all up!

SHE ATE BABY BEAR'S SOUP

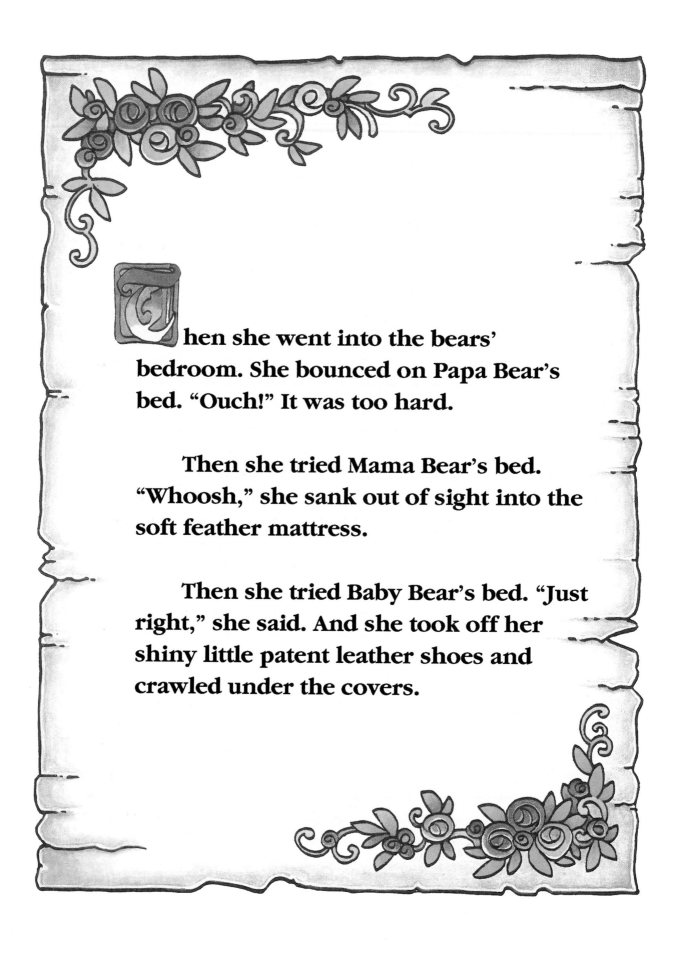

hen she went into the bears' bedroom. She bounced on Papa Bear's bed. "Ouch!" It was too hard.

Then she tried Mama Bear's bed. "Whoosh," she sank out of sight into the soft feather mattress.

Then she tried Baby Bear's bed. "Just right," she said. And she took off her shiny little patent leather shoes and crawled under the covers.

BABY'S BED WAS JUST RIGHT!

efore long the three bears came home from their walk.

"Someone has been sitting in my chair," growled Papa Bear.

"And someone has been sitting in *my* chair," said Mama Bear.

"And someone sat in *my* chair and smushed it," cried Baby Bear.

"Someone has been eating my soup," said Papa Bear.

"And someone has been eating *my* soup," said Mama Bear.

"And someone ate *my* soup all up," cried Baby Bear, and ran weeping to the bedroom.

THE 3 BEARS RETURN HOME

omeone has been bouncing on my bed," said Papa Bear.

"And someone smooshed down my feather bed," said Mama Bear.

"And that someone is snoring in my bed," cried Baby Bear.

Then all three bears growled their most fierce and noisy and beary growl.

Afrotina woke up to see three big, hairy, frowning, grouchy bears around her.

AFROTINA SAW 3 GROUCHY BEARS

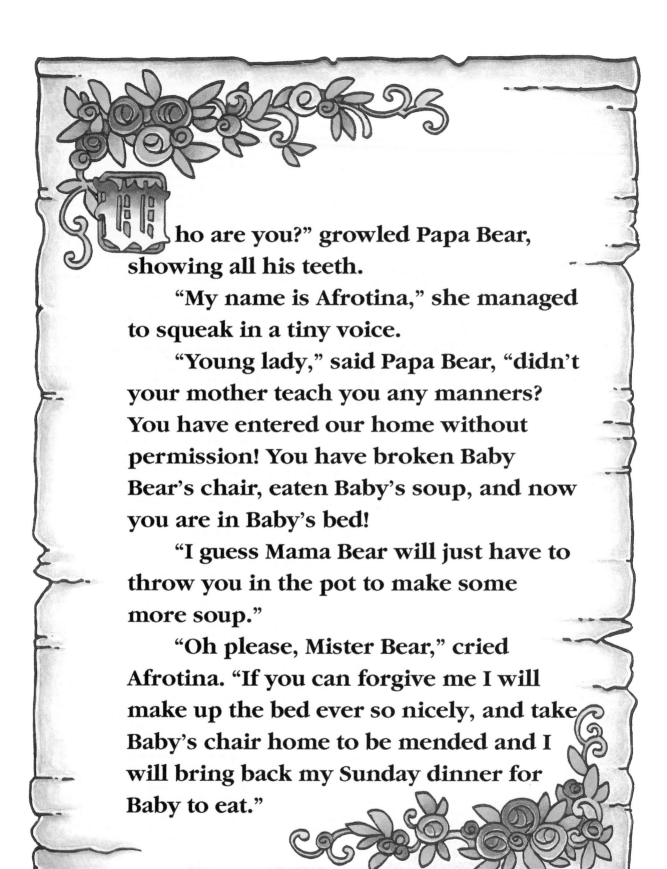

ho are you?" growled Papa Bear, showing all his teeth.

"My name is Afrotina," she managed to squeak in a tiny voice.

"Young lady," said Papa Bear, "didn't your mother teach you any manners? You have entered our home without permission! You have broken Baby Bear's chair, eaten Baby's soup, and now you are in Baby's bed!

"I guess Mama Bear will just have to throw you in the pot to make some more soup."

"Oh please, Mister Bear," cried Afrotina. "If you can forgive me I will make up the bed ever so nicely, and take Baby's chair home to be mended and I will bring back my Sunday dinner for Baby to eat."

PAPA BEAR GiVES A LECTURE

"Very well," said Papa Bear, "but if you do not return, I will come find you and chomp you all up!"

"Me too," said Baby Bear, wiping away a tear.

So Afrotina ran home with Baby's broken chair, wailing all the way.

SHE CRIED ALL THE WAY HOME

After she told Mom and Pop about her bad manners and the bears, she asked *very* politely for their help.

So her father repaired the chair, and her mother packed a lunch basket. "And this time remember, Afrotina," said her father, "Pretty is as pretty does."

"Yes, Papa," she said, and ran down the path carrying the chair and Baby Bear's lunch.

REMEMBER YOUR MANNERS

hen she came again to the bear's cave she remembered to knock. (And her knees were knocking a little, too.)

"Come in," said Papa Bear in his nicest voice.

"Oh, my chair is all fixed up," laughed Baby Bear.

And Mama Bear said, "Why, there is enough lunch in the basket for all four of us. Will you stay and join us?"

So Afrotina had lunch with the three bears. And when she left she remembered her manners.

"Thank you for the nice visit," she said sweetly, and made a little curtsey.

THEY SHARED A PICNIC LUNCH

ome see us again," said the three bears, waving good-bye.

And she did.

TRADITIONAL FAIRY TALES

Retold and Illustrated by
Fred Crump

Mgambo and the Tigers

Beauty and the Beast

Hakim and Grenita

Thumbelina

Mother Goose

Cinderella

A Rose for Zemira

Little Red Riding Hood

Sleeping Beauty

Jamako and the Beanstalk

Afrotina and the Three Bears

Rapunzel

Rumpelstiltskin

The Ebony Duckling

**A New Dimension in Fairy Tales for Children
Start Your Collection Today!**

CALL OR WRITE:

TO SOW THE FALLOW SOIL

Winston-Derek Publishers, Inc.
Pennywell Drive • P.O. Box 90883 • Nashville, Tennessee 37209 • 1-800-826-1888